For Rebecca and Naomi

First American edition 1995 published by
Ticknor & Fields Books for Young Readers
A Houghton Mifflin company, 215 Park Avenue South,
New York, New York 10003.

First published in 1995 by Frances Lincoln Ltd. London, UK

Manufactured in Italy
The text of this book is set in 24 pt. Gill Sans
The illustrations are cut paper reproduced in full color
10 9 8 7 6 5 4 3 2 1

LIBRARY OF CONGRESS CATALOGING-IN-PUBLICATION DATA
Davenport, Zoë.   Mealtime. / by Zoë Davenport
p. cm. — (Words for everyday)   ISBN 0-395-71536-9
1. Food—Miscellanea—Juvenile literature.
2. Tableware—Miscellanea—Juvenile literature.
[1. Food. 2. Tableware. 3. Vocabulary.] I. Title
II.Series: Davenport, Zoë. Words for everyday.
TX355.D345 1995   641—dc20
94-20820 CIP AC

WORDS FOR EVERYDAY

MEALTIME

BY ZOË DAVENPORT

TICKNOR & FIELDS BOOKS FOR YOUNG READERS

NEW YORK 1995

place setting

fork

spoon

plate

knife

egg

shell

yolk

white

eggcup

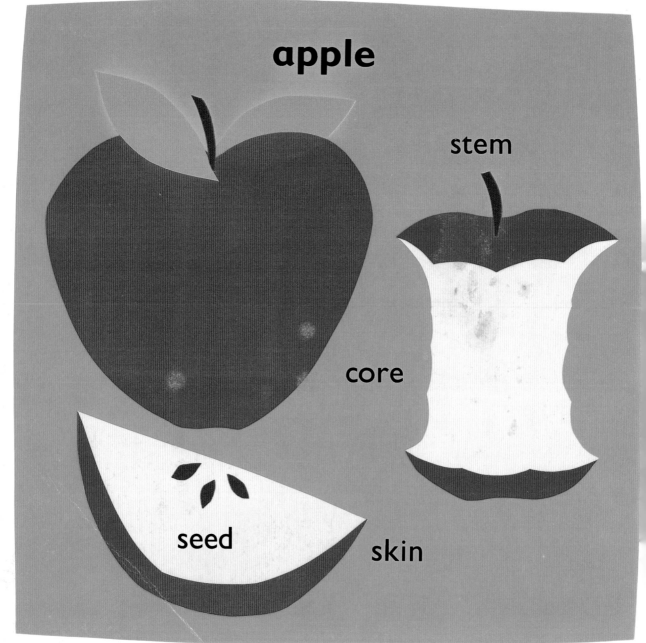

sandwich

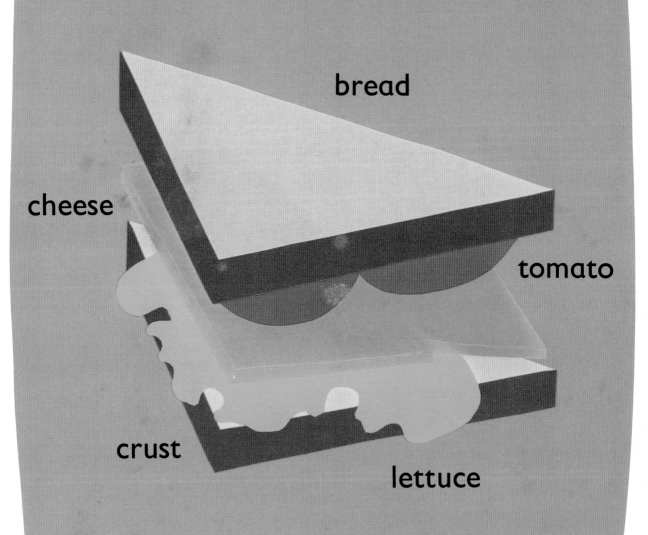

bread

cheese

tomato

crust

lettuce

cereal

cornflakes

milk

bowl

spoon

fruit

pear

lemon

pineapple

banana

orange

juice

straw

glass

orange juice

cake

frosting

cherry

chocolate

slice